AND A DEER FRIEND

First published in Great Britain by
HarperCollins *Children's Books* in 2020
HarperCollins *Children's Books* is a division of HarperCollins*Publishers* Ltd,
HarperCollins Publishers
1 London Bridge Street
London SE1 9GF

The HarperCollins website address is
www.harpercollins.co.uk

2

ISBN 978–0–00–840826–8

Ben Fogle and Nikolas Ilic assert the moral right to be identified
as the author and illustrator of the work respectively.

A CIP catalogue record for this title is available from the British Library.

Printed and bound in England by CPI Group (UK) Ltd, Croydon, CR0 4YY

MIX
Paper from
responsible sources

FSC
www.fsc.org

FSC™ C007454

This book is produced from independently certified FSC™ paper
to ensure responsible forest management.

For more information visit: www.harpercollins.co.uk/green

MR DOG

AND A DEER FRIEND

BEN FOGLE

with Steve Cole

Illustrated by Nikolas Ilic

HarperCollins *Children's Books*

Mr Dog's tree stump

The Ember Track

The Manor

The Deers'
Forest

Paddock

Storm's
Field

Cornfield
Farm

About the Author

BEN FOGLE is a broadcaster and seasoned adventurer. A modern-day nomad and journeyman, he has travelled to more than a hundred countries and accomplished amazing feats; from swimming with crocodiles to rowing three thousand miles across the Atlantic Ocean; from crossing Antarctica on foot to surviving a year as a castaway on a remote Hebridean island. Most recently, Ben climbed Mount Everest. Oh, and he LOVES dogs.

Books by Ben Fogle

MR DOG AND THE RABBIT HABIT

MR DOG AND THE SEAL DEAL

MR DOG AND A HEDGE CALLED HOG

MR DOG AND THE FARAWAY FOX

MR DOG AND A DEER FRIEND

To Edie and Alby

Chapter One

COLD PAWS AND FROZEN HOOVES

It was a cold, cold early morning in the south

of England. The full moon shone in the black

sky, casting silver light over fields of thick snow.

On the top of a hill that looked out over a frozen

lake, a tree stump was quietly snoring.

At least, that's what it sounded like.

The stump, which had once been a mighty oak tree, was hollow. An animal had found shelter inside, and was curled up tightly in a shaggy bundle.

This animal was a raggedy dog named *Mr Dog*. He had scruffy dark fur and a shiny black nose, and a red spotted handkerchief round his neck. His front paws and muzzle were the colour of snow. They twitched as he dreamed of his many adventures spent roaming the land as a free animal.

'Help!' came a sudden cry in the distance. 'Help me, somebody, please!'

At once Mr Dog's eyes snapped open under

big bushy brows. 'Someone's in trouble!' he cried.

'I can't ignore a cry for help. Dear me, no!'

He stuck his snout outside the tree stump. It was dark, so there wasn't much to see besides the snow. He couldn't smell anything either.

'That's funny,' said Mr Dog. 'I normally have such a sensitive schnozzle. So why can't I smell whoever's in trouble?'

'Help!' came the cry again.

Luckily Mr Dog also had extremely expert *ears*. They told him that the calls had come from somewhere out on the frozen lake.

And from the sounds of splashing, that lake wasn't completely frozen . . .

'Hold on, I'm coming!' barked Mr Dog. He hared out of the tree stump and down the hill.

The snow chilled his paws and left his shaggy tummy cold and wet but he took no notice. The cries for help were growing louder.

As he reached the edge of the moonlit lake Mr Dog looked wildly about. On the far side a small, dark shape was bobbing up and down through a jagged hole in the ice. 'H-h-h-help!' came a shivering cold cry through chattering teeth. 'I c-c-c-can't get out!'

Like a shot, Mr Dog raced across the frozen surface of the lake. He trod as lightly as he could – in case he fell through the ice too! – and as he drew near he had his first clear view of the helpless animal, lit by the moon's silver spotlight.

'It's a deer!' Mr Dog cried. 'A young fawn in distress!'

The fawn's head dipped beneath the black icy water and she spluttered. Her long ears were pricked and her huge dark eyes were filled with fear.

'Mr Dog to the rescue!' he woofed. Digging his claws into the ice, he leaned forward and closed his teeth as gently as he could on the back of the fawn's neck. Then he pulled with all his

strength and hauled her clear
of the water. Skinny legs
kicking wildly, the
fawn slithered
out on to the
ice. She lay
there in a pile
of pondweed,
shivering.

Gently Mr Dog put his head to her flank and
pushed her away from the hole in the ice. He
understood now why his sensitive nose couldn't
get much of a whiff – fawns had no smell until
their scent glands developed. He lay down

close beside her, sharing his warmth. The fawn snuggled up against him.

'Thank you,' she sighed.

'You're very young to be out by yourself,' said Mr Dog after a while. 'What's your name?'

'Bobbin,' said the fawn weakly. 'Did you say your name is Mr Dog?'

'That's right. D-O-G – I think it might stand for Deeds Of Goodness, which is why I do good deeds!' Mr Dog smiled. 'Tell me, Bobbin. What were you doing out on the ice?'

'Looking for my mummy,' said Bobbin, her nose twitching. 'I've been looking for her for ages. I know I should've gone round the lake

8

instead of across it. I just didn't think.'

'Well, *I* think we should both get off this ice,' said Mr Dog firmly. 'Shall we go?'

Bobbin nodded. 'I think I can walk now.'

Wobbly at first, the little fallow deer got up. Her fur was grey with white spots like snowflakes that had stuck. She started off across the frozen lake and Mr Dog watched with surprise: Bobbin walked with a curious but very sweet bobbing motion – up-and-down, up-and-down – like she was almost dancing on the ice.

Mr Dog scampered along beside her. 'You're quite a mover, Bobbin!' he said.

Bobbin's head drooped as she reached the snowy bank. 'I know I walk funny,' she sighed. 'But you see, all deer learn to walk by watching their mummies . . . and my mummy only has three legs.'

Mr Dog smiled, understanding now. Bobbin bobbed along as she might if she had three legs as well.

'Mummy had an accident before I was born,' Bobbin went on, explaining. 'She brought me up in a field by myself, so I thought that this was the way all deer walked!' She looked at Mr Dog with wide sad eyes. 'Then I met other deer and

they all made fun of me.'

'I'm sorry to hear that,' said Mr Dog. 'But the way you walk is extremely charming. Don't let anyone ever tell you any different.'

'That's what Mummy used to say,' said Bobbin sadly. 'Oh, Mr Dog, I have to find her. She's been gone for weeks!'

That's a long time to be missing, thought Mr Dog worriedly. He put on a smile for Bobbin. 'Never fear, little deer! I shall help you search.'

Bobbin beamed. 'You will?'

'What are friends paw? I mean, *for*!' Mr Dog chuckled. 'It's nearly light. Come along – let's start looking!'

Chapter Two

BATTLING BUCKS

The rosy morning sun brought a sparkle to the snowy landscape. Mr Dog followed Bobbin as she bobbed across the fields and joined a winding road. Now and then a big car would come grumbling through the slush, and the animals had to shelter under the bare

hedgerows that lined the way.

'I'm looking forward to seeing where you live, Bobbin,' said Mr Dog.

Bobbin pulled a face. 'Why do we have to go there? Mummy's not there.'

'I know she isn't. But she *used* to be,' said Mr Dog. 'So I thought that was the first place we should go to hunt for a lead.'

'A lead?' Bobbin looked surprised. 'You mean, so you can be taken for a walk?'

'Not that sort of a lead!' Mr Dog shuddered. 'I mean, one of your fellow fallow deer might have seen your mum. Perhaps they can point us in the right direction. After all, a three-legged deer

should be easy to remember. What's her name?'

'Betty,' said Bobbin.

They padded on through the snow for more than an hour. Mr Dog could hear Bobbin's tummy rumbling, and wondered where they might find some breakfast. *Perhaps in that forest up ahead,* he thought.

Then he noticed a sign above the hedgerow:

PRIVATE ESTATE
NO TRESPASSING
BY ORDER OF THE
LORD OF THE MANOR

Mr Dog could smell deer very clearly. 'Is this where you live?' he asked.

'Yes.' But the fawn seemed forlorn as she pushed through a gap in the prickly hedge. 'I'm afraid the forest isn't looked after very well.'

Mr Dog soon saw what she meant. The forest had been stripped almost bare. Shrubs and flowering plants had been cropped down to the soil. There were thick scratches in the tree trunks where every last scrap of bark within reach had been torn away. Mr Dog couldn't see a single sapling to suggest that new trees were being planted.

An angry groan sounded from close by. It

was answered at once by an aggressive grunting noise.

Bobbin froze. 'Sounds like a fight!'

Mr Dog dropped down to his haunches and crawled like a shaggy commando through the snow and fallen leaves to see. Sure enough, two fallow bucks, reddy-brown with white spots, were slowly circling each other. Each had enormous antlers, like big bony trees sprouting from their heads. Suddenly one lowered his head and charged at the other. With a terrific clatter their antlers bashed together

as each strained to push the other back.

'What are they fighting about?' Mr Dog
wondered aloud. 'Any idea, Bobbin?'

But Bobbin was no longer there.

Mr Dog looked around. Then he saw her.
While the bucks were distracted, she had been
creeping towards a long twig lying in the snow.

'Of course!' Mr Dog realised. 'There's so little
food they're fighting over it. And while they're
busy battling, that cheeky Bobbin is helping
herself to the prize!'

But Mr Dog wasn't the only one watching her
now. The bucks had noticed too.

The bigger of the bucks broke off his battle and

swung round to face Bobbin. 'Hey! Stop eating that!'

'It's a free forest!' Bobbin retorted. She quickly
chewed off the end of the stick.

With an angry snort the second buck pushed
past his opponent and charged at Bobbin. She
gave a squeal and tried to spring aside. But the
buck twisted his head and his antlers hit Bobbin
like a strike from a shovel. She was sent tumbling
through the snow and leaves – straight towards
Mr Dog!

With a yelp of surprise Mr Dog leaped up into
the air as Bobbin crashed into his hiding spot.
He landed neatly in front of the dazed little deer.
'Ta-daaaa!' he said with a bow. 'I should have

been an acrobat. Or an acro-*dog* anyway!'

The two bucks stared stonily at him.

Mr Dog gave a big doggy grin. 'Do please forgive my friend – she didn't mean to steal your breakfast.'

'Yes, I did!' cried Bobbin.

'Shhh,' Mr Dog told her, and turned back to the bucks. 'She is very hungry, you see.'

'We're all hungry,' said the biggest buck. 'There are too many deer in this forest, and the new lord of the manor doesn't help us at all. He hasn't planted any new growth in ages.'

'I'm sorry to hear that,' said Mr Dog. 'But, instead of fighting, why don't you share what you have?'

'Why don't *you* mind your own business?' growled the buck.

'Sorry,' said Mr Dog politely as the two deer stepped towards him. 'We're looking for someone,' he went on. 'A doe named Betty.'

The smaller buck snorted. 'The one with three legs? I heard the lord of the manor got rid of her. Who wants a three-legged deer?'

'I DO!' bellowed Bobbin. 'That's my mummy you're talking about!'

She rushed past Mr Dog and threw herself at the buck, striking his side with her hooves.

'Why, you pint-sized little prancer!' roared the buck. He brought down his antlers on Bobbin's head and – **CRACK!** She fell to the forest floor and lay still.

'Leave her alone!' barked Mr Dog. He raced round the bucks and ran in and out of their legs, trying to distract them. But a hard hoof kicked out and smacked against his ribs. Mr Dog flew through the air and crashed against a tree.

Dazed, Mr Dog could only watch as the two deer turned back to Bobbin.

Chapter Three

THE FIELD OF MEMORIES

M r Dog struggled to his wobbly paws as the bucks bore down on the little fawn. Their necks were pushed out and their heads low. They were going to scoop Bobbin up with their antlers and simply toss her away!

But suddenly Bobbin jumped to her feet.

She'd only been pretending she was hurt! She kicked her hind legs in a blur of speed and sent snow flying into the bucks' faces! They reared up, spluttering, hooves waving wildly.

'Run for it, Bobbin!' barked Mr Dog.

The fawn wasted no time, doing just that –
and she raced away with her bouncy lopsided
run. Her tail was raised and swishing from side to
side like a little white flag. The sight of it helped
Mr Dog follow her through the snowy forest.
Behind him he could hear the bucks clattering
after them. Other deer in the forest were spooked
and startled as the pair hared past. Mr Dog
puffed and panted apologies as he tried to keep
up with Bobbin.

A tall peeling fence blocked the way ahead.
Bobbin glanced back at Mr Dog as she ran. 'We'll
be safe on the other side of this!' she cried. 'Jump!'

And, with an enormous leap, Bobbin cleared
the one-and-a-half-metre fence in one bound!

Mr Dog skidded to a snow-scattering stop.
'Wow! That was a splendid idea – and a
splendidly *high deer*!' He tried to jump the fence
too, paws scrabbling at the wood.

It was no good. The fence was too high.

Behind him he could hear and smell the bucks
drawing nearer.

Mr Dog was about to charge off again and try
to give them the slip when he noticed
a small hole in the bottom of the
fence. He flung himself at it, but
there wasn't quite room to wriggle

through. Desperately he dug deeper into the frozen mud. Just as the bucks burst through the trees behind him, Mr Dog sucked in his sides and pushed himself through the hole and into a small snowy paddock. Moments later, the fence shook as the angry bucks slammed their hooves against it. One of the fence panels almost split apart.

'We'll be back,' grumbled the biggest buck.

'Splendid,' said Mr Dog cheekily. 'Next time it's your turn to be "it"!'

He heard the bucks stomp away and gave a sigh of relief.

Bobbin rushed over. 'Mr Dog? Are you all right?'

Mr Dog nodded. 'That buck hoof hurt my ribs but nothing's broken.'

'I think my *heart* is broken, Mr Dog,' said Bobbin, gazing around sadly. 'This used to be my mummy's field. I was born here. Now . . . it's empty. It's like those bucks said – the new lord of the manor just didn't want her.'

Mr Dog got up and licked Bobbin on the side of her face. 'Why don't you tell me the whole story?'

'All right.' Bobbin sat down beside Mr Dog and took a deep, quivery breath. 'Mummy said the old lord of the manor was a nice man. When she got out on to the road and lost her leg in the accident, he paid the vet to make her better. He

tried releasing her back into the forest but some of the deer bullied her because she was different. It was hard for her to get enough food.'

Mr Dog nodded sadly. 'What happened?'

'When I came along he kept us safe here in this paddock. In just a week I was moving about like her,' said Bobbin proudly. 'There was plenty of food just for us. We were very happy. But then the old lord of the manor left and a new man came. He said he needed the field . . . and we were in the way.'

'What an unpleasant human!' Mr Dog put a gentle paw on Bobbin's hoof. 'What happened then?'

'He turned me loose into the forest all by myself.' The fawn stared down at the snow. 'I was smaller then. I couldn't climb the fence, but I spoke to my mummy through it. Then one day . . . she stopped speaking back. She was gone.'

Mr Dog gave a soft whine of sympathy. 'A mother deer shouldn't be kept apart from her young,' he said. 'You belong together. And I'm

going to do all that I can to see that you are reunited.'

Bobbin stared at Mr Dog with her wide dark eyes. 'You mean . . . you will still help me? Even after you got hurt by those bucks because I rushed in without thinking?'

Mr Dog nodded. 'I'd like to help those bucks too, if I can,' he said. 'I'm sure they're only in such a temper because there are too many deer and not enough forest.' He licked his chops and got up. 'I think I shall pay a visit to this new lord of the manor. Humans talk to each other about all the silly things that they do. Perhaps I might overhear something useful.'

'Can I come?' said Bobbin.

Mr Dog thought of the angry bucks in the forest and shook his head. 'I think it might be best if you stay out of sight for a while! Wait for me here.'

With a cheery wag of his tail Mr Dog crossed to the other side of the paddock and squeezed through a gap in the fence where a plank was missing. He saw a trail of smoke rising up above the forest. Someone had lit a fire on this freezing day.

Now I know where to find the lord of the manor, thought Mr Dog. *And when I do perhaps I'll find some answers too!*

Chapter Four

VISITORS IN THE NIGHT

Mr Dog crept cautiously through the manor's private estate. He didn't want to run into the angry bucks again. Ordinarily he could expect to smell them coming, but right now his nose was overwhelmed with the scent of deer. He had never found so many cooped up in one forest before.

'No wonder there's not enough food to go round,' he muttered. 'Whatever is this new lord of the manor thinking of? The number of deer living here has got out of hand.'

He reached a fence made from wood and wire netting. Like everything else in the forest, it hadn't been looked after. Finding a spot where the netting had come away, Mr Dog pushed his way through on to a wide snow-covered lawn and trotted across to the long, winding driveway that snaked round the manor house – an imposing old stone building with large windows and huge arch-shaped doors.

There were lights on inside. The lord of the manor was in.

Mr Dog circled the house, looking for an open window. He longed to jump in and have a nose about! Round the back he found the food-recycling bin almost overflowing and helped himself to some tasty titbits. He gulped up some snow too, letting it melt to water in his mouth to satisfy

his thirst. Then he resumed his search for a way in. **No luck!**

As the pale sun edged towards sunset, Mr Dog was ready to give up. Then the noise of an engine caused his ears to prick. He scampered round to investigate.

A shiny black Range Rover was rumbling towards the manor.

Mr Dog watched as it stopped outside the front door and a short, stocky man got out. He rang on the bell. A tall man with a neat beard opened the door.

'Hello, Martin,' said the stocky man. 'How are you doing, my old friend and lord of the manor?'

So, the new lord of the manor is called Martin,

Mr Dog noted.

'Good evening, Mr Bedderbrite,' said Martin.

'I was just about to start dinner.'

'Great,' said Mr Bedderbrite with a grin. 'We can eat and then go over the plans. I want to make sure you're completely happy with what I have in mind.'

Martin opened his front door and waved the shorter man inside. 'So long as I can't see anything from the grounds, Joe, you can do what you like.'

The door closed behind them.

'Plans, eh?' Mr Dog growled softly. 'I think I'd better listen in and see what those plans might be!'

Night settled, dark and silvery over the manor and its grounds. Mr Dog sat outside the kitchen door with one ear raised while Martin made

the evening meal. 'I'm afraid the cook I've hired doesn't start until next week,' he said.

The man called Joe chuckled. 'With the money you're making on this deal, you'll be able to hire as many cooks as you like!'

So Martin is getting a lot of money, thought Mr Dog. *What's going on here?*

The two humans left the kitchen to dine and discuss their plans. Mr Dog raced round the outside of the house to the dining room, hoping to overhear their conversation. But the windows and curtains were closed against the cold night, and even his quick canine ears couldn't catch more than a mumble.

Suddenly Mr Dog heard an animal creeping through the bushes towards him. He spun round. 'Who's there?'

'Have you seen any worms?' came a deep voice from the darkness.

Mr Dog got up, shook snow from his belly and peered into the night. A long black-and-white animal with a stripy head was peering around.

A badger!

'Hello, there, badger,' said Mr Dog politely. 'It's not good weather for hunting worms, is it? They burrow deep down when the soil freezes over.'

'Very inconvenient,' the badger agreed glumly. 'I don't normally come this close to the house, but Martin throws away a lot of scraps . . .'

Mr Dog smiled sheepishly. 'Indeed he does. I'm afraid I've already helped myself.'

The badger sighed and drooped his head.

'However,' Mr Dog added quickly, 'he's made a meal this evening so I'm sure there'll be plenty to tuck into later!'

'I doubt it,' said the gloomy badger. 'I recognise that car. It belongs to Joe Bedderbrite, the builder. He's a big hungry fellow. Oh! Poor me. There won't be much food left after *he's* eaten . . .'

Mr Dog raised a bushy eyebrow. 'Joe Bedderbrite's a builder, is he?'

'Oh yes,' said the badger. 'He's buying the manor forest from Martin. He's going to build new houses on it.'

'He's *what*?' woofed Mr Dog in alarm. 'What about the deer?'

'If they've any sense, they'll leave before the bulldozers come along!' The badger sighed. 'Now, if you'll excuse me, I must take a look at those bins . . .'

Mr Dog was left speechless as the badger beetled away. The forest was to be flattened? No wonder it wasn't being looked after.

'Those poor deer,' he muttered.

Suddenly there was rustling in the bushes and a noisy, rasping barking started up. Mr Dog realised it was a doe! She had two fawns with her, both crying out in fear and excitement. He knew that does were very protective of their young.

Sure enough, the doe was chasing the poor badger away.

'Get away from my fawns!' she shouted.

'I'm not bothering you!' the badger grumbled, bundling past Mr Dog. 'You shouldn't be here anyway. How did you get out of the forest?'

'We broke through the fence, looking for food!' the doe bleated, stamping her foot. 'Now, clear off!'

Mr Dog saw the porch light come on. 'Please, everyone, keep the noise down!' he woofed. 'Martin has heard you. What if he—'

Comes out, Mr Dog had been going to say. But Martin had already shoved open the front door

and was marching outside – holding a shotgun!

The badger wiggled away at speed and Mr Dog ran for cover – but the doe and her fawns seemed rooted to the spot with fear.

'You dreary deer!' Martin shouted. 'I'm going to get rid of you all!'

Chapter Five

FOLLOW THE FAWN

Before Martin could raise the shotgun, Mr Dog jumped up at him. The lord of the manor fell on his side in the snow.

'Sorry about that!' woofed Mr Dog. 'But the D-O-G in my name could possibly stand for *Don't Own Guns!*' He charged over to the doe. 'What are you waiting for? Run, before he gets up!'

By now Joe Bedderbrite the builder had come out too. He helped Martin to stand, who brushed the snow from his clothes.

'This way, everybody!' Mr Dog ran off along the driveway, and the doe and her two frightened fawns followed.

Mr Dog waited for them at the fence to the forest. 'Are you all right?'

The doe stayed some way back, but nodded.

'Yes, thank you. I'm sorry to make so much noise.'

'I know a doe is very protective of her little ones,' said Mr Dog. 'That's why I feel so bad for poor Bobbin, who lost her mother. Did you know Betty?'

The doe nodded. 'I tried looking after Bobbin when she came into the forest and poor Betty went away.' She nuzzled up to her young fawns. 'But it's hard enough finding food for these two and myself, let alone any extra.'

Bobbin needs her own mother in any case, thought Mr Dog. He bowed his head to the doe. 'I hope you find some food, my *deer.* Do steer well clear of the manor house, won't you? I have a feeling that Lord Martin is *not* in a good mood!'

The doe looked pensive. 'What did he mean, he was going to get rid of us all?'

Mr Dog was about to tell her that the whole forest was in danger. Then he closed his mouth. The facts would only frighten the poor doe. She would spread the word to the other deer and soon everyone would be panicking.

Things are hard enough already, thought Mr Dog. *I will keep my muzzle zipped until I think of a way to help.* He nodded to himself and set off through the forest. 'It's high time I got back to Bobbin,' he murmured instead. 'She must be wondering where I am!'

Mr Dog yipped his farewells to the doe and her fawns, then hurried away through the freezing forest. There seemed to be fewer deer about than there had been.

He soon found out why.

The paddock where he'd left Bobbin was now knee-deep in deer! They had broken in through the split in the fence. Now they were everywhere, cropping the snowy grass and tugging at any undergrowth within reach.

'Bobbin?' called Mr Dog. 'Where are you, Bobbin?'

The bucks he'd run into before looked over, still chewing on what was left of an old shrub. 'Bobbin?' said the biggest buck. 'That little twig-stealing squirt?'

'She ran away when we knocked down the fence,' said the other buck. 'We could smell lots of lovely things growing here. Why should she have it all?'

Mr Dog harrumphed. 'Which way did she go?'

The bucks pointed with their antlers to the far side of the snowy field. Padding over to look, Mr Dog could see markings made by Bobbin's

dainty hooves – her dancing trot made the trail very distinctive. Clearly she had jumped this high fence as easily as the last.

Bobbin must have gone looking for her mum again, Mr Dog realised.

He tried to climb the fence himself but it was too tall.

I need a helping hoof, he decided.

He barked at the nearest buck. The buck frowned and wandered over.

Mr Dog jumped on to the buck's back and used it as a springboard. With one mighty flying leap he cleared the fence and landed in a snowdrift.

'Ooof. Success!' With a grin Mr Dog climbed out of the drift and shook off his fur. The countryside looked magical and mysterious, moonlight reflecting off the snow. A row of tracks led away from the fence – each hoofmark with the two narrow slots of a fallow deer.

Mr Dog put his nose to the ground and followed the fawn's tracks through the night. He trotted over fields, ducked under hedgerows and even crossed a couple of frozen streams. Sometimes he found the trail had been trampled by other animals, and he had to cover the land in sections until he picked it up again.

Hours passed. Then, as the sun began to rise,

the snow began to fall in slow white flakes.

'Oh NO!' cried Mr Dog, racing to follow the

little sharp-edged prints before they were buried

in the snowfall. But the gentle drift was soon a

fast flurry of whirling whiteness. Mr Dog could

hardly see his own nose in front of him, let alone

anything else!

Uncertain now, he peered about for the tracks, darting one way then another. His heart was sinking.

'It's no use!' Mr Dog whimpered as the snow went on falling. 'I've lost the tracks, and I've lost Bobbin too – maybe for good!'

Chapter Six

STORM THE STALLION

The snow came down for an hour or more. Mr Dog sheltered under a bush until the flakes finally slowed and stopped. Then he pushed out his nose, stretched and shook himself.

'I can't give up now,' he said, and moved off in

the direction Bobbin had last taken. 'I told that fawn I'd help her find her mother, and I am a man of my word . . . or, rather, a dog of my woof!'

But as Mr Dog carried on his way he felt far from hopeful. The sun came out and the white fields glittered in its light, but there was no one in sight, and he felt suddenly lonely.

The snow was up to his tummy and it was hard work to walk through. So when Mr Dog saw a quiet country road running beside a field he decided to take it so he could move faster. He trotted on, ears pricked for the sound of approaching cars, and for the far-off cries of a fawn in trouble.

What he heard was the laughter of human children.

Mr Dog found a boy and a girl standing on a side road that led to a farm. The boy held a sledge, but the girl had a phone in her hand. She was pointing it at something in the field in front of them, and they were both giggling.

I wonder what's so funny? thought Mr Dog, and scampered over to see.

There were four horses in the large field – three mares and a large white stallion. And the stallion was snorting and stamping his hoof at a small and unwelcome visitor . . .

'Bobbin!' barked Mr Dog in surprise. '*There* you are!'

'Isn't that fawn just so sweet?' cried the girl as Bobbin dashed past the stallion and helped herself to a mouthful of hay from a snowy bale. 'She runs like she's dancing.'

The boy nodded. 'We should tell Dad she's in our field,' he said. 'You know, she reminds me of

that three-legged doe they've got at Cornfield Farm.'

Mr Dog's ears shot up in the air so fast they almost flew away. 'Three-legged doe?' He jumped up at the boy, tongue lolling. 'You mean Betty? She lives around here? You've seen her?'

But of course the boy couldn't understand – he just saw an excited dog bouncing and woofing. 'Where did you spring from?'

'I can't even begin to tell you,' said Mr Dog. 'I must go and tell Bobbin what you've just told me! Good morning!'

'Ha! Now a dog is joining in the chase!' The girl laughed. 'I can't wait to post this video

online. It'll get *so* many likes . . .'

But Mr Dog could see that the stallion did *not*
like Bobbin! The horse was watching out for his
mares – and Bobbin had snuck into their field
to help herself to their food. Now the fawn was
dancing about dangerously close to the stallion
as he tried to chase her away.

Mr Dog flew across the field, kicking up
clouds of snow. 'Bobbin!' he shouted. 'Whatever
are you doing?'

'Go away!' snapped Bobbin.

Mr Dog blinked and skidded to a stop. 'I beg
your pardon? I've been looking for you . . .'

'You left me all alone!' cried Bobbin, upset.

'And then those mean
bucks came to the
paddock. *Everyone*
leaves me. But . . .

I don't care! I've
decided I'm going to
have to learn to look
after myself.'

The stallion interrupted with an angry whinny.

'You're going to have to learn some manners,'
he corrected her, ears flattened to his head.

'How dare you come into my field, spooking

my mares and taking our food!'

'I asked for the food but you told me to leave!'

Bobbin retorted. 'Why should I? It's a free

countryside!'

'Er, Bobbin, that hay doesn't grow here naturally like in the forest,' Mr Dog tried to explain. 'The horses' owner leaves it for them! You can't just help yourself.'

The stallion rounded on him, nostrils flaring. 'And who invited YOU into my field?'

'I'm just trying to sort out a misunderstanding.' Mr Dog sat down in the snow and gave his most winning doggy grin. 'What's your name, sir?'

'Storm,' said the stallion.

'A fine name for a fine horse!' Mr Dog bowed his head. 'I'm Mr Dog and I'm a friend to all animals. Please forgive young Bobbin here. She has lost her mother. There's no one to

tell her what's right and wrong.'

Storm whickered and turned to Bobbin. 'Is this true?'

Bobbin sighed and nodded her head.

'However!' Mr Dog's eyes shone. 'I may have found a clue. Tell me, Storm, do you happen to know of a place called Cornfield Farm?'

'Cornfield Farm?' Storm turned to a dapple-grey mare. 'Wasn't that near your old place?'

'Yes.' The mare pointed her tail to the west. 'Cornfield Farm is less than a mile that way.'

'Thank you so much!' Mr Dog ran up to Bobbin, panting with excitement. 'See those children over there? They were admiring the way

you move – it reminded them of a three-legged doe they'd seen at Cornfield Farm!'

'A three-legged doe . . .?' Bobbin boggled at Mr Dog. 'That could be MY MUMMY.'

'Indeed it could,' Mr Dog agreed. 'So what are we waiting for?'

After bidding the horses goodbye, Mr Dog found himself running to keep up with his deer friend. Bobbin was bobbing even higher than usual as she ran, fizzing with excitement. 'I'm sorry I was rude to you, Mr Dog. I really thought you'd left me.'

'I was trying to learn all I could from Martin, the lord of the manor . . . his builder friend, Joe

Bedderbrite . . . and a badger.' Mr Dog stopped running for a moment, catching his breath. 'I'm afraid it wasn't good news.'

'Oh?' Bobbin raced about in a dizzy circle, then flopped down beside him. 'What did you find out?'

Mr Dog looked sadly at Bobbin. 'I'm afraid that Martin is selling off your forest. It will be cleared, and human houses put up in its place.'

'Really?' Bobbin stared. 'But what will happen to all the deer?'

'I don't know yet.' Mr Dog shivered. He didn't tell Bobbin that hunters liked to shoot deer, and that butchers sold deer for food. 'Don't worry,

Bobbin. I'm sure your mother will think of a good *i-deer* with us to help your fellow fallows!'

Bobbin brightened. 'Do you really think my mummy's at the farm, Mr Dog?'

He grinned. 'There's only one way to find out!'

Chapter Seven

THE DISAPPEARING DEER

Mr Dog and Bobbin travelled onwards through the fields of white. The sun was climbing into the sky. Melting snow dripped from the tree branches around them as they reached a path beside a fence.

Breathlessly Mr Dog ran along the path until

he saw a sign half revealed by the thaw. He wagged his tail to brush the rest of the snow clear – and gave a bark of happiness.

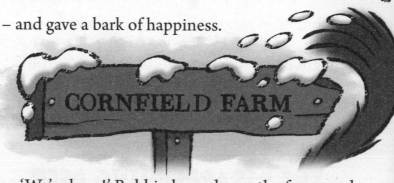

'We're here!' Bobbin leaped over the fence and bobbed about in little excited circles. 'This is the place, this is the place!' She accidentally bashed into the farm's letter box. 'Whoops!'

'Now, wait a moment, Bobbin,' said Mr Dog firmly. 'There will be lots of humans on this farm. They might not be pleased to see a dog and a deer trespassing on their property.'

Bobbin looked puzzled. 'So?'

'You must stop rushing into things,' Mr Dog told her. 'You crossed the ice because you thought it was quicker and got in trouble. You picked a fight with those bucks in the forest and it nearly ended badly. And you upset those horses in their own field – and one of them could've hurt you.'

Bobbin skittered to a stop and sighed. 'You're right, Mr Dog. I *do* rush into things. I don't dare stop to think of the dangers – because if I did, I'd never do anything at all! You see, without my mum around I feel scared all the time. I *try* to act like I'm really brave, but . . . I'm not.'

'Bravery isn't just a matter of not being frightened, you know. Bravery is when you feel afraid but you do something anyway.' Mr Dog smiled. 'You're a small fawn who's done a very big thing – you left your forest to find your mum all by yourself. You don't need to act like you're brave – you've already proved it.'

'Thank you.' Bobbin nuzzled her nose against Mr Dog's furry face. Then, as she pulled away, it twitched. 'Oooh, Mr Dog. I can smell something.' She smiled. 'It's my mummy's scent, I'm sure of it!'

'You can?' Mr Dog sniffed the air quickly. 'Hmm. I think I can detect a deer is near too!'

Bobbin almost turned a somersault in excitement. 'So what are we waiting for?'

Mr Dog led the way, pit-patting steadily through the snow. The farm, like its name suggested, was for crops not for farm animals; people in the fields were drilling for winter wheat and spreading silage. Behind a grain store were several pens and paddocks. Mr Dog could smell alpacas . . . but while his nose held the doe's scent, something didn't feel quite right about it.

Suddenly he realised: the scent was not fresh. It was at least two days old.

'One of those paddocks is my mummy's!' Bobbin burbled happily. 'I just know it!'

Mr Dog knew it was a deer's paddock too. Or,

at least, that it *had* been a deer's paddock.

Now the paddock was empty.

'Where's my mummy?' Bobbin looked about,

confused. 'I can smell her. Do you think she's

being kept inside because of

all the snow? Yes, I bet

she's in one of these

barns . . .'

The alpacas,

tall and with a

bay black fluffy

fleece, mooched

over. 'Forgive me, I

couldn't help overhearing. My name is Jess. Are you looking for Betty?'

'Yes!' Bobbin bobbed about in a circle. 'Have you seen her?' He blinked and stopped moving. 'What are you looking at?'

Jess was smiling. 'You must be Betty's little fawn. You look just like her. And you certainly *walk* just like her. You must be Bobbin.'

'I am!' Bobbin looked set to burst with happiness. 'Nice to meet you, Jess!'

Mr Dog grinned. 'However did Betty end up here? She was living in a field over at the manor . . .'

Jess lowered her head and spoke quietly in

Mr Dog's ear. 'I did hear that the new lord of the manor was going to sell Betty off for venison! Well, the farmer's wife, Carys, heard about this and said *she'd* take the poor deer. She loves animals, does Carys. She works as an Open Space Officer . . .'

'A who-what officer?' said Bobbin, leaning in.

'The farmer's wife helps look after the countryside,' Mr Dog translated.

'Countryside Carys, we call her,' Jess agreed. 'You know, she's furious that silly old Lord Martin is trying to sell his forest to builders.'

'So are we!' said Bobbin.

'But where *is* Betty?' asked Mr Dog.

'I'm afraid she's gone.' Jess looked down at the ground. 'Betty stayed here for a couple of weeks. But the first chance she got, the night before last, she sneaked out and left the farm.'

'Left?' Bobbin gasped and sank down to her knees. 'Why would she go?'

'She told me she simply *had* to find you,' Jess explained. 'Being without her Bobbin was breaking her heart.'

'And . . . being without her is breaking *my* heart!' Bobbin looked at Mr Dog with tears in her eyes. 'If Mummy's out looking for me, she could be anywhere!'

'She left two nights ago,' Mr Dog pointed out.

'Surely the first place she would have gone was the forest.'

'But we asked around yesterday and no one had seen her,' said Bobbin.

'True...' Suddenly Mr Dog gasped. 'Wait! She left on the same night that *you* were out looking for *her*. Perhaps she picked up your scent before she even reached the forest...'

Bobbin gasped. 'And she tried to follow it, but now she's lost?'

'I'm sure she'll turn up,' Jess said kindly.

'Countryside Carys has spread the word, asking people to watch out for her. Ooh, look, here she comes now.'

A tall, glamorous woman wrapped up in a winter coat came bustling out from behind a barn. 'I need the pickup truck!' Carys shouted. 'Someone thinks they saw our runaway doe down near the Ember Track. I'm going to check it out.'

A man working in a field called back. 'The keys are on the kitchen table, love. Call me if you find her.'

'Don't worry, I'll call everyone!' Carys declared. She turned and hurried away.

Mr Dog nodded to the worried fawn. 'All right, Bobbin. Get ready to follow me as carefully and quietly as you can. If Carys is going to look for your mum, we're going with her!'

Chapter Eight

TRAPPED!

'Take care, pets!' said Jess the alpaca as Mr Dog and Bobbin stole stealthily away. 'Hope to see you again!'

'I hope so too,' said Bobbin.

'With Betty beside us!' Mr Dog added.

He and Bobbin scampered through a barn and

hid behind a grain silo. Ahead of them stood the farmhouse. Parked beside it was a dirty green pickup truck. There was a snow-covered canvas stretched over its back.

'With luck we can hide in there,' Mr Dog told Bobbin. He dashed over with the fawn bobbing along beside him. Luckily the canvas was loose at one corner. Mr Dog jumped up and arched his back under the material – which was stiff and freezing cold – to make the opening as large as possible for Bobbin. The fawn scrambled under the canvas

and tried to make herself some space among ropes, containers and other bits of junk. Mr Dog cringed – Bobbin was making a lot of noise!

Finally she lay quietly on her side. Mr Dog snuggled up beside her for warmth. 'Carys said that Betty had been seen near the Ember Track,' he recalled. 'Do you know what that is?'

'No,' Bobbin whispered. 'I just hope she's really there.'

The crump of footsteps in the melting snow carried through the canvas. Mr Dog felt the truck lurch as Countryside Carys got inside, then the chug of the engine made the floor beneath them rumble. Moments later, the truck pulled away.

'Here we go then,' Mr Dog murmured. He looked at Bobbin, wide-eyed and trembling. He hoped more than anything that the young fawn would soon be reunited with her mother. But what about all the other deer back at the forest – what would become of them if their home was sold for development?

For once Mr Dog didn't know what he could do. He felt helpless, and it wasn't a happy feeling.

The journey was slow with so much snow and slush on the roads. The going grew bumpier and slower still, as if the pickup was driving over rough land. Eventually it came to a halt.

Mr Dog stuck his head out from under the canvas. Bobbin stuck her head out beside him.

The pickup had brought them to what looked like a very old railway line surrounded by towering fir trees. Scrubby brambles grew over the rusty tracks. Piles of old timber had sprouted moss and mushrooms. Old train carriages lay tilted at angles on gravel slopes.

Spindly trees grew up around them.

'Now I understand why this place is named Ember Tracks,' said Mr Dog. 'It must be for the rusty rails. They're the colour of embers.'

'I think I recognise this place,' said Bobbin. 'I came here looking for Mummy the night I met you, Mr Dog!'

Suddenly, through the sharp Christmas smell of the firs, Mr Dog detected a definite odour of doe. 'Bobbin! There's a deer near here!'

'What?' Bobbin jumped down into the snowy grass. 'Mummy?' she called. 'Are you there?'

'Bobbin . . .?' A weak cry carried through the crisp air. 'Help!'

'That's her!' Bobbin darted away, dancing over the brambles, skidding through the snow. 'Mummy! I'm coming, Mummy!'

'Wait for me, Bobbin!' Mr Dog leaped down from the truck and raced to catch up with the fawn as she climbed to the brow of a slippery slope. Birds of prey slowly circled high overhead.

'Mummy!' Bobbin squealed in alarm. Then she vanished from view over the top of the slope.

'Bobbin, no!'

Mr Dog put on an extra surge of speed. To his relief he found that the fawn had only gone forward a few steps.

But his doggy heart plunged as they looked

down and saw Betty all
tangled up in a rusted fence at
the bottom of the slope! She
was jammed between two train
carriages, their roofs stacked with
iron spikes and baseplates and old
planks of wood used for fixing down

the track. Several mouldering telegraph poles had fallen round Betty, trapping her tight. Two more remained precariously on the slope, like battering rams pointing straight at her.

Bobbin was trembling. 'I didn't rush in, Mr Dog. I remembered what you told me about thinking of the danger.'

'You did very well, Bobbin,' said Mr Dog proudly. 'If you *had* rushed in there, you might have brought those poles rolling down and made things worse.'

'Bobbin!' Betty struggled feebly against the fence, trying to get to her fawn. 'Bobbin, I tried to find you!'

'I'm here now, Mummy!' said Bobbin, her voice shaking. 'And I've brought a friend to help!'

'Mr Dog at your service!' He stood on his hind legs and raised a paw. 'What happened?'

'I was out looking for Bobbin,' bleated Betty. 'I thought I saw her dancing up here so I came . . .'

'I *was* here, Mummy!' Bobbin called.

'I must've missed you. I slipped in the snow . . . got tangled in this old fence on the way down.' Betty shivered and sighed. 'I tried to struggle free but the poles were tangled in the fence too and they almost fell on me . . .'

'We will get you out, Mummy!' Bobbin turned to Mr Dog. 'Won't we?'

'Of course we will, Bobbin,' said Mr Dog. But inside he was worried. Betty had been stuck here in the freezing cold for two days already. It would take time and experts to get her free, and the doe was already weak.

How much longer could she last?

Chapter Nine

TO THE RESCUE!

'We can't get Betty out by ourselves,' said
Mr Dog. 'We'll need some help – from
Countryside Carys!'

Bobbin smiled. 'She's looking for Mummy too.'

'And she helps to look after open spaces in
the countryside,' Mr Dog recalled. 'She's bound

to know people trained in helping and handling injured wildlife. I'll call her now.' He scrambled back to the top of the slope, threw back his head and howled as loudly as he could.

Carys came into sight from behind some trees. She looked puzzled to find a dog woofing at her.

'Please, madam, kindly come up here!' Mr Dog barked. But Carys couldn't understand him, of course. 'All right, change of plan – Bobbin, get bobbing about. Carys has never seen you before – but I'm certain she'll recognise that wonderful walk of yours!'

Bobbin beamed. 'Because it's just like Mummy's! You're brilliant, Mr Dog.'

Mr Dog woofed in what might have been cheeky agreement. Then Bobbin did as he'd suggested, parading on the slope in her distinctive wobbling way.

Carys gasped. 'That adorable little fawn moves about just like our runaway doe!' she cried. 'What's going on?' Slowly, not wanting to spook the fawn, she climbed up the slope to investigate.

Finally she reached the top – and gasped to find Betty far below.

'Oh, you poor darling,' Carys said. 'How are we ever going to get you out?' She pulled out her phone and pressed some buttons. 'Hello, it's me. Put me through to our animal welfare unit . . .'

A long, quiet minute passed. Carys began to pace up and down on top of the slope. 'Hello? Yes, I'm out at Ember Track. I'm going to need a vet on standby – whoops!'

She slipped and nearly fell. Her foot sent a flurry of large stones sliding down the slope. They struck one of the delicately balanced timber poles – and it rolled towards Betty!

'No!' Bobbin cried.

'It's all right,' barked Mr Dog. 'It's going to miss her!'

He watched as the timber slammed into the old carriage to the left of the weakened doe. But the force of the crash shook the unsteady stack

of planks, spikes and metal baseplates piled on
the carriage's roof. The pile teetered on the edge,
ready to drop on Betty's head . . .

'Oh no!' breathed Carys, holding still.

Betty and Bobbin closed their eyes.

Mr Dog held his breath, trembling.

The debris on the roof stayed put.

'Yes, I'm still on the line,' Carys spoke quietly into the phone, as if afraid a loud word might cause the other pole to slide down. 'Now, I need a team to come out here urgently. Call Bedderbrite too – Ember Track is his property, after all. He needs to see that it's not a safe place for wildlife . . .'

Joe Bedderbrite again! thought Mr Dog. *It seems he causes nothing but bother.*

'You need to shoo, you two.' Carys waved Bobbin and Mr Dog away from the slope's edge. 'One wrong move and all that junk could come crashing down on our darling doe.'

A gust of wintry wind blew across Ember

Track. Bobbin moved closer to Mr Dog. 'How long will we have to wait for someone to help Mummy?'

'I don't know.' Mr Dog was watching the red kites circle high above. 'I'm just afraid that if a bird lands anywhere near the carriages, it could bring the whole pile of wood and rails crashing down.' Mr Dog looked at Betty, still lying with her eyes closed in the tangled fence. He took a deep breath and came to a decision. 'Bobbin, I'm going to try to get your mother free.'

Bobbin blinked. 'But how?'

'With these!' He held up his front paws and bared his teeth in a doggy grin. 'After all, a dog

can squeeze into places that people can't.'

'Good,' said Bobbin. 'What can I do?'

'Stay talking to your mum,' Mr Dog urged her. 'You have a special bond. Keep her strong. Tell her she mustn't give up!'

With that Mr Dog padded down the safe side of the slope. He circled round behind the carriages and crept carefully over rubble and rubbish and waste. Betty lay ahead of him, a forlorn figure half buried in the snow.

Mr Dog walked towards her, into the shadow of the debris poised to fall. He saw Bobbin watching his progress keenly from the top of the slope.

'Mummy!' Bobbin called. 'Don't be afraid. My friend Mr Dog is just behind you.'

'A dog?' Alarmed, Betty tried to struggle up. 'I'm scared of dogs . . .' She kicked out a leg and the wire fence scraped against the side of the carriage. A spike dropped down from the roof, thumping to the ground between the doe and Mr Dog.

Mr Dog flattened his ears. 'Hold still, Betty!' he cried.

The deer did so.

'Mr Dog won't hurt you, Mummy. I promise,' Bobbin called. 'Trust me.'

Betty stopped her struggles. 'All right . . . I do trust you.'

'Thank you, Betty,' said Mr Dog, edging closer. He could see clearly now how the doe had got tangled up. If he could just gnaw through two of the wooden fence posts, then he could free her front legs – then dig a trench in front of her so she could crawl out to safety.

'You know, some say the D-O-G in my name stands for Daring Old Gent . . .' Mr Dog swallowed hard. 'Here's where I get to prove it!'

Slowly, softly, he crawled in beside Betty.

He felt her breathing come fast and shallow. As carefully as he could he closed his jaws round the thick rotting wood beside her front hooves and began to chew.

'That's it, Mummy! Stay nice and still.' Bobbin went on calling down encouragement. 'The vets will be here soon . . .'

The wind blew harder. A magpie settled on the carriage roof – then flapped away as one of the old wooden planks slid off and hit the ground behind Betty.

Mr Dog worked on grimly. How long did they have until the whole lot came crashing down?

Chapter Ten

THE FATE OF THE FOREST

Mr Dog kept chomping at the old wood, spitting splinters as he worked. He went on chewing until the first fence post broke apart with a dull snap.

'Now for the next one,' he muttered. He moved his jaws round the second post and

worked them like scissors.

Tense minutes passed. Crows cawed as an east
wind chilled the air. But eventually the second
post snapped like the first.

'Very slowly, very carefully, try to pull your
legs clear,' Mr Dog told Betty. 'I'll see if I can dig
us an escape route under this wire . . .'

The frozen ground was hard going. He clawed at it, clumsily at first, clearing clods of earth from in front of Betty as she freed her legs. Birds still circled overhead and the wind grew stronger. But Mr Dog kept calm and kept on digging, and slowly the trench deepened. When it was deep enough he crawled under the tangle of wire – but he knew that Betty was much bigger. He dug as quickly as he dared, afraid that any vibration would disturb the debris above.

'Mr Dog!' Bobbin shouted, dancing away from the top of the slope into some nearby bushes. 'More people are coming!'

'Give them my best regards!' panted Mr Dog,

all his concentration on the job in hand – or, rather, the job in paw.

Glancing up, he saw Carys had returned with a man and a woman in green uniforms. He supposed they were the animal welfare unit. Behind them stood stocky Mr Bedderbrite the builder – with a boy and a girl who also looked familiar.

Of course, Mr Dog realised. *Those are the children I saw at Storm the Stallion's field, filming Bobbin!*

'The trench is nearly ready,' Betty bleated. 'I can't thank you enough, Mr Dog!'

'Once will do very nicely.' Mr Dog smiled and

kept on burrowing. 'But only once you're out of here!'

'I don't believe it!' the man in the green uniform exclaimed from the top of the slope. 'That dog is doing our job for us!'

'I think you can get out now, Betty.' Mr Dog backed away. 'Very, *very* slowly – very, *very* carefully. Try it!'

Although she was weak and groaned with the effort, Betty edged forward. Keeping herself as flat to the ground as possible, she worked her front legs and head into the trench and pushed herself through with her one back leg.

'She's doing it!' called Carys – as a creaking

noise came from the carriage roof.

'Look out, Betty!' barked Mr Dog. 'That old junk is going to fall!'

Desperately the doe wriggled all the way under the wire. Mr Dog reared up and pushed her clear. Then *he* ran too as the wood, baseplates and rusting spikes came crashing down right where she'd been lying.

'Mummy!' Bobbin burst from the bushes and bounded up to Betty. 'Thank goodness you're safe!'

'Bobbin!' New strength seemed to flood into the weary doe at the sight of her fawn. 'I've found you at last!'

Mr Dog grinned as the two deer began to race and bob about the slope together. They came together to box and nuzzle, then danced about again, free and happy. The animal welfare officers laughed to see the display, and Carys clapped her hands with joy.

The children giggled. The girl was filming the dancing deer on her phone!

Mr Dog panted happily, sinking to his haunches.

Then Carys marched up to Bedderbrite the builder. 'You've owned this land for years and done nothing with it,' she told him. 'It's a hazard for animals – but if you looked after it properly, it could be a paradise for them!'

'Not this lecture again,' grumbled Bedderbrite. 'I've told you, Carys, I want to build factories on this land. I've just got to fix the drainage problems first, and that takes money. Money I'll get once I've built and sold the new houses down at Martin's manor.'

'You wouldn't need to fix the drainage problems if you let it go back to nature. Marshland would attract all kinds of wonderful wildlife,' said Carys.

110

'Let the council buy it from you so we can rewild this area. Then perhaps the poor deer losing their home in the forest can make a new one here!'

'That's a brilliant idea, Dad,' said the boy beside Bedderbrite.

'Yes, Dad!' said the girl, lowering her phone. 'You know how much I love the deer. Please say yes.'

'I'll think about it,' Bedderbrite said grumpily, and stomped away through the snow.

I hope you think about it properly, thought Mr Dog. Then he couldn't help but laugh as Bobbin bounced up and knocked him over in excitement, and Betty nuzzled her nose gratefully against his side. '*Deer* me,' he joked. 'What an adventure we've all had!'

A week later, Mr Dog was snoozing happily in the hay in Betty's paddock at Cornfield Farm.

Betty lay beside Bobbin. The mother doe had been checked over by the vet, and, aside from dehydration and some minor scrapes, she was declared fit and well. The medicine she needed was her fawn beside her, and Carys had agreed at once that Bobbin could stay on the farm as well.

Mr Dog smiled sleepily. Carys had said that she wanted to adopt him too, which Jess the alpaca had thought was an excellent idea.

'I never stay in one place for too long,' Mr Dog explained to her. 'But I'll certainly wait a while to see our deer friends are well settled here before I head off.'

Life went on quietly and comfortably, though Mr Dog couldn't help but worry how the deer in the lord of the manor's forest were getting along. Then, one Saturday, Countryside Carys gave a whoop of excitement that carried clear across the farm. She came rushing out to the paddock where her husband was working.

'These deer have saved the day!' Carys was grinning from ear to ear. 'They're an internet sensation! Bedderbrite's children posted their video online, and it went viral! Hundreds of thousands of people have watched them . . .'

'Viral?' Bobbin was puzzled. 'What does she mean?'

'She means an awful lot of people have watched you and your mother dancing for joy on their computers,' Mr Dog explained.

Betty shrugged. It was all beyond her.

'Joe Bedderbrite's girl mentioned that our little fawn here will lose her forest home when Martin sells off the manor's land for building houses,' Carys went on. 'Nature campaigners are up in arms – there have been deer on that land for five hundred years.'

'Quite right,' woofed Mr Dog.

'Anyway,' continued Carys, 'in the video's comments I posted that Joe Bedderbrite also owns the Ember Track, which would make a perfect open space for wildlife without a home ...'

The farmer smiled. 'Crafty.'

'Bedderbrite just called me up.' Carys looked flushed with delight. 'He doesn't want bad publicity, and he hates his daughter being so upset – so he's agreed to sell the Ember Track for rewilding! He's even saying he'll leave half of the manor forest as it is and sell it on to my department. We can manage it properly so deer can still stay on the land.'

Bobbin jumped up and danced about. 'Wonderful!'

Mr Dog grinned. 'And it's really all down to you and your mum and your special way of moving!'

Bobbin ran up to Carys and nuzzled her, then bounded back to her mum. 'Do you think we might live in the forest again some day?'

'I don't know,' said Betty. 'Perhaps we'll stay in this new wilderness when it's ready!'

'Or maybe you'll just stay right here with me,' said Jess the alpaca with a smile.

'We'll be happy wherever we are,' Bobbin declared. What about you, Mr Dog? Where will you go?'

'I have a choice too,' said Mr Dog. 'I can go hither or thither . . . or near or far!' He gave his biggest, doggiest grin. 'But wherever I might roam, if I see an animal who needs a dear friend – I'll be right there!'

Notes from the Author

I love watching a fawn with its mother. They have such a close and special relationship. Mostly the doe (a female deer) will only have one or two fawns, who will stay with their mother for around a year. But even when the fawns are pretty small they'll be getting ready for an independent life. The fawn will usually take its first steps within twenty minutes of being born. Then in just a few hours it will be able to walk a little further. While it's still a little wobbly on its legs and not able to go very far, its mother will lick it until its almost completely clean of any scent so that predators won't be able to find it and then the mother will hide it every day while she goes to find food. After a week or so the fawn will be ready to step out a little more on its own until it's finally ready to leave home in about a year's time. Even then,

some fawns will come back once they are grown up to join their mother in a herd. It's a happy family relationship.

The story of Bobbin and her mother was also inspired by something else, though. A few years ago I met a wonderful three-legged deer. She moved in a slightly different way – but she was happy and lively and running and jumping everywhere. I was told that she'd lost her leg in an accident but this isn't quite as bad as it would be for us. When you have four legs, losing one isn't always quite such a big deal, because a four-legged animal (or 'quadruped' to give it its proper name) can learn how to shift its weight and find its balance across three legs. The natural world has plenty of examples of three-legged deer, lions, tigers and other animals that can live in the wild, even without humans to help them. It's just another example of how amazing animals are.

Have you read Mr Dog's other adventures?

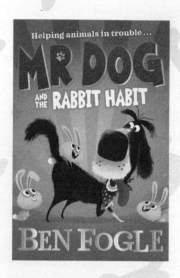

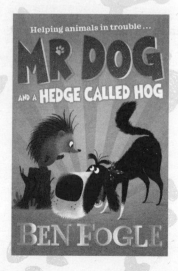

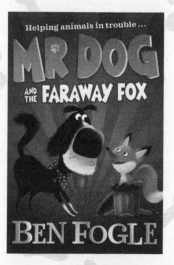